Three Clues

Written by
Jill Atkins

Illustrated by
Alex Patrick

Ransom

One day, Kirsten got a letter.

It said,

Dear Kirsten,

It's my birthday on Saturday.

Will you come and have fun in my garden at 3?

From Delroy

Kirsten grinned.

"I like Delroy," she said. "He has a big garden with fir trees at the end."

On Saturday, Kirsten got out her best trainers and a blue shirt.

Mum took her up the road. There were lots of people in the garden.

"Have fantastic fun!" said Mum.

Then Mum left, and Kirsten ran off to play
with Amal and Carlos.

Then they stopped for a drink and a snack.

"Now we'll have the best fun of all," said Delroy. "We'll play The Hunt."

"What's that?" said Kirsten.

"You get three clues!" explained Delroy.

"The first one to get all three clues right is the winner. This is the first clue: **The blackbird can have a drink.**"

"I do not understand that," said Amal.

"I think I do," said Kirsten.

She ran to a little pond at the bottom of the garden. Amal and Carlos went with her.

The second clue was next to the pond.

Do not forget to have lunch.

Kirsten frowned.

"That's a hard clue," said Carlos.

"Yes," said Kirsten. "But I think we need to go to the barbecue."

She ran across the garden. Amal and Carlos went with her.

"Yes!" yelled Kirsten. "I can see the third clue."

"It's just a map," said Amal.

"Yes, but look, there's a red cross," said Kirsten.

She looked hard at the map. Then she sprinted to the fir trees at the end of the garden.

She needed to get there first.

There was a little red cross on the ground.

Kirsten dug in the dirt until she felt something hard.

She lifted a metal box out of the dirt.

She lifted the lid and took out a Book of Clues.

"Wow! Thanks!" Kirsten said to Delroy. "I like this Book of Clues.

The next hunt will be in my garden!"

Sal the Sow

Kasia Reay

Illustrated by Alex Hoskins

Schofield&Sims

Sal the <u>ow</u> has a litt<u>er</u> of piglets.

Can you te<u>ll</u> <u>th</u>em ap<u>ar</u>t?

Tu<u>ck</u> has h<u>air</u> on his ba<u>ck</u>.

Ja<u>zz</u> has h<u>air</u> on her <u>ch</u>in.

Lill is a bit fatter.

Sid is a bit thin.

Tig has a d<u>ar</u>k h<u>oo</u>f.

Ne<u>ll</u> has a m<u>ar</u>k on her <u>ear</u>.

This is Bi<u>ll</u> wi<u>th</u> a m<u>ar</u>k on his r<u>ear</u>!
N<u>ow</u> you can te<u>ll</u> the piglets ap<u>ar</u>t...

but if they go in the mud it is f<u>ar</u>
t<u>oo</u> h<u>ar</u>d!